Alien

Fly on the Wall Press

Selected and Edited by Isabelle Kenyon

First published 2021 by Fly on the Wall Press

Published in the UK by

Fly on the Wall Press

56 High Lea Rd

New Mills

Derbyshire

SK22 3DP

www.flyonthewallpress.co.uk

ISBN: 978-1-913211-40-0

Copyright © 2021

Contents

The Strangford Stone stands over 10 metres high in Delamont Park, County Down and was created from granite from the Mourne mountains (also in County Down).

(Cover Image by John Winder)

Observing its probation period
By Holly Magill

It comes in early and stays late
to finish work it's too slow to keep up with.

We view from a distance.
Management had given us a talk on Equality.

After a few weeks its eyes are shadow-rimmed,
bloodshot. They never met ours in the first place.

Might've been pretty, those pooled hazel eyes –
if they didn't roll like a doped-up baby doll's,
and shit, those pinprick pupils.

It doesn't speak to us in the street – rude.
So mostly we ignore it.

*

It wears startling jewel colours – purples, pinks, turquoise,
strappy sandals and twirly skirts nipped in at the waist,
makes us uncomfortable with its breasts.

Yesterday, at the photocopier, it was bent right over,
wriggling to free a stubborn jam.
We caught Nathan eyeing its arse –
but he's desperate, would take what he can get.

When it stood, a fist of crumpled paper clasped like
the world's most pathetic leading lady bouquet,
someone down the far end mimed fevered applause.

Of course it was none the wiser.

We didn't mention the black toner smear on its flushed face.
We put it on reception duty the rest of the day.

Only fair.

Godstorm
By K. James D'Agostino

Someone put a box of kittens in the church donation bin and this woman's looking in:
>*At least they're only cats. Imagine if it were horses.*
>*You can see human-ness in a horse's eyes!*

And I think about when I saw God's skull in His cloud-lined coffin overhead.
Like a dented egg, It had no eye sockets, no mouth, no ears.
Since then every storm is God's skeleton churning in the sky,
turning above a woman trapped in her attic by rising floods,
or above a man gasping in his car as brown water bubbles up, and seraphim looking in:
>*At least they're only humans. Imagine if it were…*

My cats quarrel and I lift one by his scruff, pin him to my side, turn him on his back.
Light flashes in his eyes. I have seen children look like this,
predator-sleek and hungry to their bones.
Are humans never hungry for meat?
For dinner I rend a chicken's softened flesh from its fragile bones.
The cats scream around me and my wife purrs at them. She asks, as always:
>*Why are they so cute, these babies?*

and I answer, as I always answer:
>*If they weren't cute, then we would eat them.*

I wonder why they do not eat us. Does our human-ness obscure our meat-ness?
The elders would tell me the cats can see the god-ness in our eyes.
And I know, I know, there is such a thing as god-ness, but I can't
see it for all the humanity, all the meat and the pulsing blood,
all the clouds and the lightning and God's featureless skull
in the way.

Visitation
By Samuel Strathman

Shadows roam the hallway,
stopping to scratch
at my door
until they can slink in.

Smokey projections cluster
on the wall
by my bed,
creeping down low
for a story.

Snake charmer sets out
on a new mission —
forgets his prosthetic
at home.

Helsinki
By Damon Moore

The details don't matter.

I could recount the whole episode
except it would not lodge, second or third-hand
as well as the tick, burying head, shoulders and mouth-parts
as you were pondering

from the changing rooms of a smart
Helsinki clothes outlet, that possible summer dress,
finding, cosy between both breasts a creature
already investigating.

Instantly losing interest in new outfits,
we rebounded into the contusion of copy-cat infractions,
roving misdemeanours
such as being arrested in Madrid for looking suspicious

or detained on Paris Métro in possession of a double-punched ticket.
It is not unjust, ticks hitching a ride
for a visit to Helsinki,
and could happen to any native Finn or guest of one.

But we got out of that store in a hurry,
which is symptomatic of how life goes on
through surgeries of daily events, shudders of arrival,
gathering new information at stopping-off points,

finding your way around with the minimum of fuss,
a welcome like snow when it comes
soundless and serene, the changing room curtain drawn back,
flight from a tick, the freezing of the Baltic.

Home
By Allie Kerper

Home

the legitimate aim
of maintaining effective immigration control.

is so wholly lacking in substance

The Three-Armed Woman
By Allie Kerper

The three-armed woman can't decide
which arm to tattoo first.

The three-armed woman has incredible wanks.

The three-armed woman marks papers efficiently,
although she can only read one at a time —
two arms type comments
while the other holds the Diet Coke.

The three-armed woman
never hears strange men
talk about her tits.

The three-armed woman has a very happy dog.

The three-armed woman eats veggie burgers
without the patty falling out the back.

The three-armed woman flips off
whomever she wants.

The three-armed woman has never tried to juggle,
and donates to a mutual aid fund
each time someone asks.

The three-armed woman reads clickbait
about octopuses escaping their tanks.

The three-armed woman hears strange men tell her
what she should do with the extra hand,
and she punches them in the face.

The three-armed woman is a superhero
in the eyes of most small children
and also her friends, though when the latter say it,
they mean in the everyday way
of kindness and impossible strength.

The three-armed woman gives really,
really good hugs.

Nocturne
By Jean Gillespie

Is it from the velvet
resonance of whale song
or the dark timbre of wolves
howling vibratos to other selves?

The Earth has a song,
All the planets do -
You can listen on the NASA website,
To those far-distant melodies

Messengers, ringing out through
Dead-space, caught in the
Tendrils of life, The Earth,
A nightingale among the stars

All whirling and booming a light-song
Refracted, detected, recorded.
Magnetic blooms holding them fast
Light-waves their lines of gravity
Heartbeats in an ocean of time

Sailing against the void.
On screen, I watched the trace and track
Of a particle deep underground
From that 26-mile bunker in a borderland,

Somewhere,
A faint luminescence.
Then looked outside at the night
And thought of you.

Epistle
By Jean Gillespie

Late afternoon, winter 2004

We sat, three of us
hunched, shadowed in a slopped and tethered coal-black hut;
on a rotting, rope-strewn shoreline

Waiting for the battered kettle's whistle to shriek
from the stove (the only light) spewing forth a brew
of withered tea leaves swimming in beakers to warm our cupped hands.

Old men, you and your guest.
As talk of fishing and war falters, inspiration leaks out the sodden walls
and the small, pinched face of the visitor announces
"Hitler got it right with the Jews".

We two stare, dumb, as acrid smoke from the stove creeps into our eyes and nose
and shifting gleams light up the visitor's eyes, the spite of fanaticism tarnishing the air.
Your demands of explanation do not assuage the guest.

We look down at our boots, damp and wrinkled, coded silence for the night is over.
It is a relief to leave the gloomy, ugly shack into the clear night
But as I turn towards the sea to damp down the malodorous air,
I am instead, caught by a scene of beauty that takes my breath away.

The sky strikes a tone, a chord of perfect blue, a harmonic vibration so pure
that the sea reverberates like a bell, its echo shimmering like a forgiveness.
I want to reach out and touch through, grasp the transcendence

I see you, my friend, draw the sight into yourself and know you are thinking
of the Antarctic and the clean bright walls of colour dancing over the ice
a sight never forgotten.

The visitor does not notice though. "These are moleskins - real moleskins"
he says smoothing down his trouser leg.
And I thought of the little satin black velvet creature of childhood
frantically heading for safety, nose-down into a tunnel.

Sally's Little Friend
By Lee-Ann Coleman

Kate was woken by the doorbell ringing. It wasn't the polite, single bell signalling a delivery, but a continuous, furious pressing. Looking down from her first-floor bedroom she could see Sally, her neighbour, bouncing from foot to foot outside the front gate. Kate pulled on her robe and rushed down the stairs to let her in, reaching the locked gate and fiddling with the catch. Sally in her bathers, dripping from her swim, hair matted to her face, looked a sight. She was so agitated, that Kate was scared. With the gate finally open, Sally rushed through, screaming,

"Get it off, get it off me!"

That was Kate's introduction to Sally's little friend.

"Sally, stop, you have to calm down and let me see," shouted Kate, as Sally's distress transmitted itself to her. Sally sat, her wet bathers making a damp patch on Kate's rather nice sofa. Getting to her knees in front of Sally, Kate leaned forward so she could look at whatever it was wrapped around Sally. Neither of them wanted to touch it.

"It looks like a jellyfish," said Kate. "Maybe it's more than one, or the tentacles have somehow gone all the way around your body. Does it hurt?"

Sally's breath was still ragged, but visibly calmed by Kate, who, amazingly, wasn't as horrified as her. Sally nodded, her perfectly manicured nails hovering over the thing. "It stings but it's tingling, like an electric current. I don't know - my muscles are jumping and, weirdly, it actually feels quite nice."

"I think you may be in shock," Kate exclaimed, trying to hide her disgust. How could it feel nice? She'd never seen anything like it. It seemed gelatinous, but it looked tough, more like plastic than jelly. She went and got a wooden spoon and touched it, gingerly. The strands, wrapped around Sally's torso just under her breasts, contracted, making Sally gasp. The fabric underneath the strands of her one-piece swimsuit had dissolved and the thing was in direct contact with her skin. In the middle, it was elongated and domed, almost like a head, poking up between her breasts. Sally was looking down at it when the bulge pulsed and got bigger. The head was losing its transparency, becoming milky and opaque. Two patches on either side of it were getting darker and slits were forming. Sally and Kate watched silently, unable to comprehend what they were seeing. Suddenly, the slits quivered and, with a wet plopping sound, they separated to reveal two large sea-blue eyes staring up at Sally.

"Oh, my," said Sally, softly, "aren't you gorgeous."

Kate let out a strangled cry and fell in a slow-motion heap on the floor.

After extensive medical investigations, the doctors concluded that they were unable to do anything for Sally. Her companion had integrated with her body to the extent that removing it would kill her. Besides, Sally had no intention of being separated from it – she called it BooBoo - a development many found almost as shocking as the thing itself. Scientists didn't know what it was, but used terms like *parasite* and *xenomorph*. Sally knew her little friend, her BooBoo, was nothing like those aliens. Although they had told her – and shown her the images – that the creature had not only wrapped around her body but had penetrated it as well. Sally had read horrifying examples of the damage that parasites could do to their hosts but she'd never felt better. She felt like a new woman.

Her husband, Rob, a tactile man who loved giving Sally a hug, no longer did so. In the beginning he'd tried to hold her, but BooBoo's head would stretch up, its eyes would open and swivel around to stare at Rob. It was off-putting, to say the least. Sally would laugh and say, "I don't think BooBoo likes you as much as I do, Rob." She realised that she no longer liked Rob as much as she once had either and BooBoo provided a convenient barrier to contact with him. In bed, Rob had tried different approaches but there was no avoiding BooBoo, always there with them. Their sex life, already on the wane, dried up completely. Sally, despite her shows of sympathy, was secretly pleased when Rob went to sleep in the spare room.

Sally had taken to wearing V-neck tops so that she could see BooBoo. Rob would watch Sally staring down between her breasts into the creature's eyes. It was revolting. As she could no longer wear a bra, the whole effect was unappealing. After her initial reluctance to touch BooBoo, Sally now stroked its head all the time. She wouldn't touch him, her husband, but she lavished attention on the foul thing. She'd always been so 'put together' – her clothes and hair immaculate and her figure enhanced by the right underwear, which she'd spent a lot of money, Rob's money, on. Now she didn't bother with makeup or the hairdresser, although she was still beautiful in a wild sort of a way. And when she wasn't touching BooBoo, she had taken to staring off into the distance.

"What are you thinking, what's going on?" asked Rob, confused, as his wife became silent and contemplative.

"Oh, nothing," Sally would reply, with a smile.

And while Rob might have believed that Sally didn't think about much beyond her next shopping trip before BooBoo attached itself to her, he knew that she was lying now.

Her neighbour Kate had become distant too. They'd been friends from the time Sally and Rob had moved in next door. Now, Kate couldn't quite make eye contact and no longer suggested they go for a coffee or a walk along the beach. Sally didn't mind – she spent a lot of time walking or swimming on her own – well not really on her own as BooBoo was with her. Before BooBoo, her days had been filled with shopping and appointments – the hairdresser, the beauticians and seeing friends for lunch. Now she couldn't stop thinking about everything. How had the wonder of the world passed her by?

At the beach she'd walk, marvelling at the feel of the sand between her toes, considering the trillions of grains, the millions of crushed creatures that she would never know the names of. In the water, she could feel the presence of beings great and small. Floating on her back, Sally could see the stars even in the day, feel the spin of the earth, its place in the solar system, at the edge of the Milky Way, slowly rotating. Although BooBoo didn't have a mouth, it was communicating with her all the time. They had a secret language. She realised she'd never loved anything or anyone as much as she loved BooBoo.

Then, one morning, she woke up and BooBoo was gone. She'd reached between her breasts to stroke it as she always did and there was nothing there. She emitted a long, loud wailing cry of loss and despair. Rob, who hardly ever went into their old bedroom, rushed in to find Sally tearing frantically at the bed sheets, searching for her BooBoo. Rob, seeing she was free of the thing, felt elated. He grabbed her, trying to calm her down and, once she'd stopped crying, made her sit on the bed. Only then did he realise that BooBoo hadn't gone, as Sally looked up at him with her new, sea-blue eyes.

Unzipped
By Claire Walker

After I gave birth to my daughter, while I lay cradling her in the crisp clean
sheets of a maternity bed, my body grew a new me. With one
long exhale, my skin unzipped and out she slid, quiet and instinctive.
Because she knew how to hold the girl; was so sure of this fresh employment,
my baby and I thrived; made friends with ourselves and those like us.
This new me felt at sweet ease with teaching how to feed, smile, how to count
on fingers, how to shape our mouths into *mama*.

At thirteen, our certainty is delicate as sugar work. Those two, who slipped
knowingly from me, have less to say. Still entwined by blood and love,
but some days laughter halts in thickened air. The bared teeth
of that zip pull away and come apart.
And although we remember how to smile, sometimes our mouths cloy with stuck
apologies. There is a confusion within us. Those people we once knew
not quite gone, not quite there either.

Red on White
By Nasrin Parvaz

Holding her child's hand
pregnant, panicked
she looks for her ticket
in her bag.
The police
drag her onto the white platform
in a white country.
The child is frozen
lost behind boots
watching
the stream of blood
coming out
from between
her mother's legs.

Middletown Border
By Anita Gracey

October 1983

First, they ignore you, then they laugh at you, then they fight you, then you win. - Mahatma Gandhi

In a rainbow of darkness,
brakes an Ulsterbus
I awake to curses,
then a grim silence,
my holdall throbs.

A para charges the aisle,
he snares my eye, winks,
fires a cheery grin.
I don't smile, I don't move.
I've been baptised in
be polite, don't react.
The officer directs the driver
everything is ok.

In the raving rain
I want to punch,
to soak my Irish skin,
to kick my Docs,
to scream at all.
But I resist,
as Gandhi said,
then you win,
let us pass.

To Ali at the Corner Shop
By Catherine Davidson

Ali, I lost the poem about you.
In your store, we talk tomatoes, rain.
You weigh pomegranates, say my name,
ask about my children, smile as I pay.
In your Iranian aisles I shop with ghosts
picking up kalamata like my mother,
blocks of feta, mountain oregano,
briny scents a sea to travel time,
back to her father's deli in New York,
report card pinned to the board, a child
of history growing up between languages.

That day your story spilled on the counter:
an artist roaming around with a camera,
the heavy hands that broke your freedom,
hidden under a sigh and a shrug about things
we cannot change. The cumin and lemon
air shimmered; I saw you mapping a city
white as marble, images arising like a gift,
salt sadness I stuffed into a bag, abashed.

In a poem a student shared by Gabriella Mistral,
the strangeness of strangers becomes a garden,
full of seaweed, wrack and ruin. The poet
claims loneliness turns into our last pillow,
in a world that will never know us. I thought of you,

dear Ali, and that lost poem: how each time
I greet you I hold between us a bridge of silence.

History of the English Language
By Catherine Davidson

Podcast Episode 108, 1238 AD

Cod rot in Norwich harbour:
all buyers across the water
hide from fear of plunder,
hoofbeats from the steppes,
shops shuttered, streets empty
sea-haul held, trade halted,
a hoard lost to horde rumour.

"Hoard" – to keep for oneself
from Germanic "hort"; hard T,
locked box, heavy key, secret.
"Horde": from the Turkic "ordu": O
a circle: nomads, tent flaps, horses
open plains, provisional migrations.

Dear English, did you know
you were so multidirectional?
T and O, port and plunder, east
and north, you hermaphrodite
fish, you shoal of history, you
treasure decomposing in an arbour.

Single Green Alien
By Cheryl Byrne

I'm here because you fell that time. I watched you trip and tumble down the stairs, your hair flying in all directions, like a cloud of red surrounding you. I heard the dull whack as you turned over and over, and the snap of your ankle breaking. I saw it up close from further away than you can comprehend. I saw you lying on the floor unconscious and cursed the limitations of even our technology. I was more relieved than I can tell you when you woke and struggled to the telephone to call for help. I stayed with you and watched until that help came, so you weren't alone. As impossible as it seems, there was a moment when I think you saw me. I was sure you looked at me with those beautiful eyes and I felt seen. Please, don't close them now.

I've heard humans talk about guardian angels a lot. Mystical beings that follow you and protect you. They don't exist of course, I would have seen evidence of it. But what was to stop me being yours? Or something similar anyway. I could use the technology that we have and watch over you. It was technically against the rules, we observe and study, we don't interact. But your species is so vulnerable in so many ways and you were more so than any other human I have seen. Not only physically, but your networks were dissolving around you. You were lying unconscious at the bottom of the stairs and I knew no one would find you.

So, I came to be your network. On the way here, I thought through what I would do, I could hardly knock on the door and introduce myself in my natural form, but it would take too long to synthesise a disguise and practice it. I would need to hide. The house gives plenty of space for concealment. I settled on the attic. This was back before you had the ceiling fixed and most of the house was visible from there. To begin with, it was almost the same as before. I just watched you. The first day was when you were painting the kitchen. Your ankle had healed to a point where you could walk, but I saw that you were in pain and it took a lot of effort to resist the temptation to take that pain away. You had picked a plain creamy colour and were using a roller to apply it to the wall. It stank! I could barely stand it for days after. It snuck through all the gaps and into every room in the house. I could have changed the colour without the smell, but I was glad you had started this again. You had pressed pause on the project, the fixing and decorating after she left you. I had watched her leave, you know? The crying and shouting at one another. Her confession to you, your forgiveness of her and her rejection of that forgiveness. She never deserved you. You gave her so much of everything, of yourself and she didn't appreciate that. Worse, she seemed to find it inconvenient, annoying. I must confess, when you forgave her, I shouted at you from the holoroom. I wanted to shake you, tell you not to forgive her not to give her that. I could see what was coming and she shouldn't have been able to walk away with a clean conscience.

How's my voice now? Do you think the practice is working? I think I'm starting to get the hang of it. I've got the hair colour right. The red was tough. I like the feel of it down my back, when I swing it back and forth like this and it brushes against the skin. I have never had this before, our hair is different, harsher.

I could follow you from the house. I have concealment technology, we all do, so we can study various species without them seeing us. It bends the light and makes us basically invisible. I followed you everywhere, like a good guardian angel would. I watched you at dinner with friends. Remember when the blonde one talked about setting you up? I was there, standing behind her. She looked down after she mentioned it so she didn't see the sadness and the fear. She didn't see your eyebrows contract, just a little, or that you bit your lip to keep from crying. By the time she looked back up, you had pushed it all down, but I saw it. I wanted to interfere then, to stop her from talking, from telling you about this woman who would be perfect for you. No one is perfect for you. But I restrained myself, partly to see what you would say. You said no and I was a little proud. Your friend was not. She thought you needed to move on, but I knew that you just needed some time to be looked after, to be cared for. When she talked you around, when you agreed, I nearly turned off the concealment then and there.

I think I have the eye colour now as well. The bright green that so few of you have which shines from your face. The green of nature. What do you think?

It was hard not to interfere, so much so that I would help in small ways, just to do something. I would add an item to your basket if I saw you had forgotten it in the supermarket, just little bits, tuna or cheese. I found your keys a few times, and your phone. I fixed a few minor electrical issues in the house. I guess that's how it started. I would say it was a mistake, but it's led us to this. So, when you were on the date you obviously didn't want to be on, I thought, what could it hurt? I made it rain whilst you were out, just a tiny adjustments needed. But you ran laughing into the bar with her, holding her hand. You found a table and whilst she bought drinks you ran hands through your hair and removed the black mascara from under your eyes. I could see her doing the same thing at the bar. I had thought you would just stay for a short time, but it was hours later when I pushed her drink over you. Red wine to stain your blue blouse, the one that I've seen you wear often, that you love, just to give you an excuse to leave. You assured her it was fine over her exclamations of ignorance at how it could have happened, and then you bought her a replacement.

Your behaviour was familiar, I had seen it with the last one. You were making the same mistakes that you made before, deferring to her, and always being there when she wanted you to, never saying no. You went where she wanted to go and did what she wanted to do. When you were looking forward to a night in, you went dancing because she was in the mood. If you had a craving for Chinese food, you ordered Indian for her. Her timekeeping left a lot to be desired and that annoyed you, I could tell by the way you tapped your fingers on the table, and glanced at your phone and the window. She told you not to be so uptight the first few times and then you would bury it all down and try to be more easy-going for her. You would smile and kiss her and tell her it was ok really. You were just stressed. Then, eventually, you said nothing at all.

Kisses are one of the fascinating things about your species. I sometimes wonder how it happened, who was the first person to think that pushing their lips against another pair of lips might be pleasurable. I know that's not how it works. That it would just be part of your evolution, but it is one of the stranger things you do. You get close to someone, like this, and look into their eyes. They really are a lovely green. Then press your lips into theirs. Like that. Is it about the connection? Being that close to someone physically? Feeling them with such a sensitive part of your body. My physiology doesn't give me the same sensations as you, but it's nice, all the same, the closeness.

It was the argument that made me do this. When she was so late, that the dinner you had cooked was ruined. The sauce cold and congealed and the meat burned from trying to keep it warm. When she finally arrived at the charred smoky mess, you were angry and I was elated. You would tell her, you would let her know that this was treating you badly, and if she could treat you badly in this way, then she would start doing so in other ways. You were going to demand what was your due. When you accepted her apology so easily, so quickly, I had to leave. I paced in the attic, knowing that I was making the boards creak, but I didn't care. It was infuriating! Oh, no, no don't jump like that. I won't hurt you. I would never hurt you. I'm protecting you. From yourself in a way. It's just that I came all this way to be your guardian angel and I need to stop you this time. You understand, don't you? I watched the pain the first one caused in you, I documented it in our social interaction files. That entry is truly pathetic. See? I'll translate:

"One of the pair shows desperation in how she acts, whether from fear of being alone, or from an affection that is not returned. She allows the other to determine all courses of action and does not seek confrontation under any circumstances. Indeed, she appears to go out of her way to avoid it despite showing obvious signs of distress. The more senior of the two is dismissive of the other, obviously frustrated with her subservience. She often shows a level of disdain in her facial expressions when the other is not watching."

Do you see what I mean? Do you see why I need to do this?

How do I look? Your cheekbones look great on me, don't they? They feel good. This clothing is great too. The colour matches our eyes, it was always my favourite. This really is the best way. I figured it out whilst I was pacing and you were letting her walk all over you. It's the best way to protect you. You'll be safe up here and I'll deal with her to make sure she doesn't come back anymore. I know what you deserve and it isn't her.

Wolf in Waiting
By Kevin Bateman

I had just my physical body
To start my astral body
I can travel to the past, the future and the present
To discover our irrational thoughts or actions
When we are not in control
When it is someone else moving the pieces
Destroy my other self
And fix my breathing mind
Enjoy the lamb

Yarrow Falls
By Louise Mather

To lie against the woods / the soft-shook mines
upturned treetops / tumbling / dew villanelle
unchaining my hair / with your grazed fingertips

I rest my head underneath / in the crook
once believed / the blue bright kingfisher
scuttering between / boughed-veil / electric-grift

smaller than I knew / a coin on a photograph
the bells / drawing sanctuary / enfold me
into your story / nocturne / how it used to be

before / crested blood and fossa bones
creatures with their scarlet-shank mouths
blunt-scragged hooves / unfurling plagues

to sleep / by Astrantia twilight / glamour
kindly / granulating
our words / spooling / kaleidoscopes

all that is left / less than I care for
I pick out / thorns / from your heart
hook / by / hook
gather them / under my skin

Northern Quarter Doll
By Louise Mather

Slumped crystal-eyed
with one grizzled unwieldy shoe

a tattered bouquet
of peroxide coils swamped

to purging drains
canal shunted

cobbles by witching hour
city astronomy

dress mauled
nettling innards

of cold wool and soot
a startled expression

where wires jutted
flashed glow

worms scuttling
from severed arm

frayed at the joint
a glut of nebula

abandoned
to dank alley stoop

of blue neon future
occulted potions in gems

northern quarter
by arrangement

for hollow luck to never
have uncovered

their face

By the Dozen
By Julian Bishop

They line the fridge like giant bullets,
oval interiors heaving
with avian embryos, alien formations
created out of albumen,
fatty deposits of deutoplasm -
who would ever eat that?

Born bald, excreted from a chicken's
crack, they sit forlorn
in cardboard rows, lined up
unhappy abacuses
awaiting the embellishment of bacon,
their grisly fate on a plate.

Little space invaders,
scaled-down solar systems in shells -
why do we shatter
your fragile firmaments, why do we fry
your diminutive moons
cupped around their wobbly suns?

Beaten with sugar and butter
and a shake of flour, eggs might bloom
but hens lay eggs in good faith -
not for a kitchen fry up. Other
than for chicken propagation,
I see no point in them.

Lamezia Terme
By Julian Bishop

The beach is tessellated with drifts
of burnt plants - wisps of dull
thrift, ghosts of Verbascum,
buckthorn, storm-rocked kale

sickle-shaped pods. Spider
headed spinifex is whisked
across silver-shingle grains
by winds whistling like fists

on a red-hot hob. Sea-oat,
gorse, every salt-crisped shrub
falls to its knees, sits in ash
flicked from its own rigid stub.

Wailing plovers form jagged
lines to scour pulverized shells
glittering among a litter
of charred cars, plastic bottles.

Strange visitor
By Palak Tewary

Stranger

in our midst.

Ask it – yes do.

What does it want?

Is it an enemy or a friend or   just an unknown stranger

that has lost its way and   is now as terrified of us

as we are of it? We call him   an alien. What does it call

us? Can you not ask?

Do ask - yes do.

If it tells us it's from another place – will we believe?

We will just coz it has one eye and two mouths.

And then we will alienise it just as we do those –

which are

different   race   colour

gender   religion   orientation

or simply   just different   than you

so why   should   this

outsider not be considered so utterly outlandish? -

even though it may be more terrified than we are.

lgm

By R.G. Jodah

       they are always there
slithering
       at the bottom of a glass
hanging
       beneath the shoulder
of a long-necked bottle
                          waiting
for my piss-poor defences to weaken

so they can slip in
            like wet metal
      cephalopods
           a writhing
of memory
           and otherness
and an open mouth
           screaming
into a cutting white light

The Slush Planet
By William Shaw

Before I was abducted by aliens, nobody would publish my science fiction stories. My prose was hackneyed, my characters one-dimensional, my situations unbelievable. That was what the steady stream of rejection emails said, anyway. I was on the verge of giving up for good when a beam of light descended on me from nowhere and, as I say, I was abducted by aliens.

The bridge of the spaceship was vast, filled with eerie lights and threatening shadows. The aliens appeared from the darkness, triangular eyes staring at me like a new plaything. I couldn't believe my luck! At last, the inspiration I needed to write a great science fiction story!

"Greetings, Earthling," said one of the aliens. (I didn't think aliens still said 'Earthling,' but if these guys really weren't from Earth they might have been behind the times). "We have a job for you."

*

The aliens explained everything, and they were really quite polite. They told me they represented Supernova Books, an intergalactic publishing company. They were thinking of expanding into the Earth market, but they needed a slush reader, someone to read the many thousands of submissions and determine which might be worth publishing. And of the eight billion people on Earth, they had selected me.

I told them I was honoured, and took note of how the aliens' tentacles wiggled in recognition. This would all be good material for the story I was going to write.

*

But all the stories they had me read were awful. Some made no sense, with meandering plots and impenetrable dialogue about quantum theory and star ship maintenance.

Some were offensive, with long tirades about how humans were inferior life forms, or descriptions of bodies crushed beneath alien jackboots.

But worst of all were the clichés. I lost count of all the dark and stormy planets, all the sensuous encounters with well-endowed cephalopods, all the grizzled galactic investigators motivated by dead broodmates.

It was torture to get through it all. There wasn't a single publishable story in the whole stack of submissions.

*

I was on my way to the bridge with the rejects, when I overheard two aliens talking.

"It seems that the human slush reader experiment is a success."

"Affirmative. The subject has demonstrated a 26% efficiency improvement over our original slush readers."

"Excellent. Then the Slush Planet Programme will commence. Soon the Earth and all its inhabitants will be dedicated to processing submissions."

The aliens shared a small, dry chuckle, and I ducked back into the shadows. The entire planet, forced to read *this stuff?* I had to do something.

*

So that's why I'm writing this message to you now. I just have to figure out the aliens' communication system, and then it will be sent to every newspaper, every magazine, every publishing house on Earth. The world needs to be warned. The life and sanity of every human being is at stake.

Please, you have to publish my science fiction story. Before it's too late.

The Siren Star
By Daniel Hinds

On the first day, in the place empty of it,
The spaceman cracked his nose

Till his visor did the same.

On the second, his grieving replacement
Sent out to complete the essential maintenance

Downed tools
Unlatched the white umbilic cord.

On the third day, the astronomers with their one wrinkled eyes,
And the children given a telescope for their birthdays

By parents with too much disposable income
And too few ideas, disposed of their sight.

On the fourth day, those who lived in overgrown concrete
Cities snarled and starved of light unpowered by the spark

Of their own invention, stood in the unshadowed fields
Looking up.

Like a sailor, far from shore, surrounded by nothing
And nowhere, they turn their gaze to the horizon

To see another sight, to burn away the infinite
Fields of grey and green and blue and white.

On the fifth day
There were no seeing men left.

On the sixth, no women.

On the seventh, the last man put on his suit
And left the station

His eyes sealed by the flame from his kitbag.
Even then, he was still called to see.

The citizens of the sun. Three copper women scarred
By the lines of three black holes at their necks

Sucking in starlight.

Three eyeless women, hair and gowns rippling like flags
In an impossible wind.

The ends of hard white limbs clotted black.
Exposed to empty chaos.

She lifted his heavy glass mask
And made first contact with her lips.

A pursed eclipse of dark-blooded skin bordered in bronze
And the scratch of fingers hard as metal on his Adam's apple.

From that day we took our breaths from blackness.

On Being of Polish-German Origin in England in the 60s & 70s
By Louise Longson

At first, the only thing I noticed was people
saying, 'You've got a funny name,' or, saying
it wrongly. Then, feeling, somehow, wrong
myself. Like some sneaking Jahnke,
traitorously trying to trap them in a
consonant conspiracy.

Later, I realised a funny name meant
something even funnier. No matter
whose side you were on - soldier, sailor,
rich man, poor man, refugee, Jew – it was
the G-word that was counted first in this
ill-fated plate of plum stones.

Like when mum went to the City Council
for housing and was told she should be
ashamed for asking. That there were better
people than her (and him) more deserving of
a proper home, a garden – a piece
of a bulldozered field
that is forever England.

Like when they play the G-word at a game
they might not win, struggling since Sixty-Six
not to notice "ACHTUNG!" headlines or John Cleese.
Not to mind being called 'Nazis' or 'Krauts' which –
rhymed with louts - at least lets a budding poet
display a sense of humour we
don't possess, allegedly.

Dandelion Diaspora
By Andrew Geoffrey Kwabena Moss

Proud nations given alien status
Stateless seed dispersal
The dandelion clock
Ticks, tocks and makes a wish

Blown from West Africa's shores
To the auction block
To plantations of tobacco and cotton picking
Fingers snap and find New World rhythms
In shock, millions of magical florets,
Lost
Descend then globe-trot

Golden Akan crowns bend down, disintegrate
Into silver-tufted afro puffs
Grown grey-weary with time-fate
Clocks, blowballs, ticking timebombs

Awaiting

Glorious explosion, regenerate
Puffed parachutes land
Around a pappus vortex ring of smoke
Enriching drab projects, housing estates
Sewing new treasured seeds
Rapid colonisation of disturbed soils

Continuity of bright, silky kente tapestry
Once stripped, re-stitched
Coast to coast, across
Connecting Atlantic rifts
Once sailed by slave ships

Ticks, tocks and makes a wish
The dandelion clock
Stated seed dispersal
Alien status creates proud nations.

It
By Fokkina McDonnell

Hiding it is risky.
If I get vascular dementia
I will forget where I buried it.
A dog in a fluorescent yellow jacket,
a paid-up employee
of North-West Water
sniffing out leaks,
may find it.
It will be reported in the local paper.
It will be on the national news.

If I swallow it, it may show up
on the security screen at the airport.
The staff will prod me,
they will take me away
and search me, a full body search.
Or it will burst
and I see my blood spurting out
in front of me.
My bones will fly high into the air.

Dream of a Wanderer
By Tim Kiely

after 'The Wanderer', ll. 39-50

She thought that she had seen a most rare thing
somewhere on the safe side of night.
She swore that she heard words strike sparks
off the dark, keeping her awake
through the tolling of waves on the dinghy ribs,
smacking from the crest of one abyss to the next,

'when sorrow and sleep   both together
oft bind   the lonesome wretch'.

Words that dreamed whole fingers and arms
around her children's heads; drew them close
in the bone-stripping cold when she could not;
words that kept her loving and fierce -

'then he wakes   and sees   grey waves…
fresh frost and snow   mingled with hail' -

words she can never have known, but which give
more heat than the outboard motor; give more
than what waits, officially, on the coast:
assessment for hypothermia, then arrest.

'then heavier   are the heart's banes,
sore for the one sought   sorrow renews' -

She will hold to the dream even as it burns,
brighter than the lights of Littlestone
with its heritage pubs and smiling old women
who dream invasions. She has sailed her own
long road through waters empty of whales,
washing with bodies - this endures.

44. Casts of heads of male and female Eskimos *
By Rebecca Drake

Truelove rifts
ice is an absence of
ink is the colour of ancient ships
biscuit is the colour of Inuit shoes labelled M.45.299 in a controlled
hand is the thing that thrusts, that breaks on the back of the
whale is the true leading line through the blueblack swelling, through tilted Arctic
storms are the pathetic fallacy of the
whale is the silenced
victim is frozen at the barb of
TRUELOVE's arrow is the first of many to
cut is to reduce history to bride-blushed curlicues on
white porcelain is the colour of her polar grimace.

*44. describes the contents of a case of objects pertaining to a nineteenth-century Hull whaling voyage to the
Arctic, in which objects and people were collected.
The title is taken from a 1956 catalogue for Hull's Maritime Museum.

'Tales from the Other Box' by Rick Dove, published by Burning Eye Books (2020)

Review by Tim Kiely

Paperback | 79 pages
Publication date 13 Aug 2020
ISBN13 9781911570899
£9.99

Rick Dove is one of those irritating poets whose work you will read and immediately resent for having said the necessary thing so well already. But given that the necessary things still need to be said, again and again, it's just as well they are said in such excellent poems.

'*The hardest lessons of history repeat*', Dove writes, and those repetitions break out across these poems in ways which highlight their oppressiveness and absurdity. Anyone who has heard Dove perform, and heard the rage build incrementally in his delivery, will feel it burning through the pages, especially in extended meditations on racism and how it perpetuates. Abstract notions like the law of large numbers become the sharp realities of over-policing through stop and search. Generations of Black Britons seeing their children meet with prejudice sit them down for '**The Chat**'. Another nondescript Wednesday headline shows 'black teenager *dies again*'.

Dove's flagship metaphor is that of Schrodinger's cat, simultaneously alive and dead until the box containing it is opened and observation establishes one conclusive reality. 'Lifting the Lid' practically fizzes with the clashing of racist perspectives, made even more lively by the charge of deft internal rhymes:

'… *that both co-opted and rejected me*
adopted and neglected me
that still imagines me
taking jobs while stealing welfare simultaneously'

And yet the act of opening the box, and 'making real', might also achieve something meaningful. In other poems, like 'Lensing', repetition becomes a means for looking again, for ensuring that a homeless former science teacher will not become '*invisible / as they die*' like a black hole. In 'Fatherland' the repetition becomes affectionate, even essential, as a vehicle for transmitting history, identity and connection with a slowly disappearing father figure:

'*in our last World Cup together*
this is what you taught me…
…. something mumbled about Nietzsche
about what doesn't kill you
something mumbled about stronger'

These are poems that actively encourage, not to say require, re-reading and re-appraisal. There's even the occasional abecedarian like 'History 101', a glorious riff on the '*now read bottom to top*' style of composition now much in vogue in the age of Instagram, here executed with an expert's verve.

There are times when the sheer chronological, thematic and linguistic range of these poems mean they don't always gel neatly. I certainly found myself getting jarred, and doubling back, over the odd archaic formulation like '*lest they see me*' or '*afore belittled*'. But then accepting that might just be the price of admission for also getting to pore over a bit of Internet-inflected brilliance like this:

> '*you touch nothing   because evidence*'

Dove has said in various interviews that he wants his readers to learn how to engage with other perspectives, and his poems certainly reward this kind of sustained, delicate attention. These are the kind of poems that, even as they make you sadder or angrier, will thrill you, and push you somewhere new.

'Confess: The Untold Story of Dorothy Good' by Juliette van der Molen, published by TwistIt Press (2020)

The Spellbinding Powers of Language:
Review by Benjamin Francis Cassidy

Paperback | 90 pages
Publication date 9 Oct 2020
ISBN: 9781733974455
£10.00

Dorothy Good, the title character of Confess: The Untold Story of Dorothy Good, was a real person. Her horror was real, too, and the first poem in the first section of the book does an excellent job of showing how, in ways only poetry can. Aptly named "Farewell", the poem's opening line tells why: 'a goodbye screamed'. Bang. The story begins. Immediately, the line prepares the tone. The lower-case letter 'a' chosen to represent a child's voice. But it offers more than that. The very voicelessness of this child, Dorothy Good. Four years old. The poet knows she can't possibly know the words spoken, as the child's mother was taken away. Line three does the job of showing the imagined scene, and employs guttural, raw language to give the ordeal palpable realism. It's one nobody wants to ever have to think about. But the 'howled to the rafters' sound is necessary for us to imagine. That's the point of this poem: it happened and can't be ignored. It's too dangerous to brush off as just the past, and it's utterly unjust that it has been, in many ways. That process began with the 'Puritan hands' of the final line. The poet has begun to remove them from over the mouth of Dorothy, so we can hear what we must. This is the history of a life, told through poetry.

The final poem of the first section is an ambitious one, realised with care and concern. Here, the poet uses voice powerfully to put herself in the world where the action she's concerned with takes place. The first line, 'deep in the dark' creates various effects and implications, simultaneously. The clipped, single syllables of 'deep' and 'dark' create a sense of foreboding and finality. The tightness of the language creates a sort of claustrophobia, that comes through via the utterances and accent of the vowels. Furthermore, the terms fuse concrete imagery and abstract concept. The scene described, literally, and the mood evoked. Further into the poem, there's more use of assonance to create tension, in the lines "a peek" and "a wink", set out on their own lines. And then the final line "Salem's first witchcraft pact" ends with a beginning, reversing the way the opening poem of this section began with an ending. An example of fine crafting, abundantly present in these vital poems.

Section two deals with the subsequent trauma of the accused and the consequences. Indeed, the trauma itself is part of the sentence. "Prophecy", draws on these themes and ideas, and finds ways to make them palpable. The line 'scourge of wagging tongues' is potently economical. It brings to life the real story of how things happened. It roots the violence, showing how it began, as a result of suspicion, then evolved into subsequent mass hysteria. This line puts the real culprits on trial, giving the victims a status of exactly that: victims. Crucially, the line highlights how it all started with words. Now, says the poet, we should use language to commemorate their tragic plights.

By the time the fourth and final section arrives, the horrors have been shown. Vitally, they're felt, in the reading of the poems. For example, a line in the second stanza of "Of Prayers and Spells", in the third section, speaks out from over three hundred years hence. It calls the too-late cries for help 'entreaties seeking ears,'. Their urgency and importance are made poignantly clear, as we hear of lives 'tossed about in godly storms'. The helplessness and gravity of the desperation is established. The rhythms in the line let us imagine this as a metaphor, but deeper consideration tells us that the atrocities and acts of barbarism were very much delivered by humans.

Just before the collection draws to a close, the last poem reminds us once more of the value of human life. The poem takes the form of a letter from the dead. A particularly tender element of the poem is found in the direct address to the reader. The poem is much more than an account of terror. Or a declaration of sorrow. The speaker doesn't ask to get a hearing for the sake of their own pity. The imperative command of 'You must listen' is repeated early in the poem and again around the middle of it. It becomes apparent that the voice within this poem is very much a collective one, though focalised singularly. The reader is very much involved in the poem's voice, as the speaker acknowledges that they can't force their message. They explain that 'I'm leaving a trail'. And that's exactly what the poem does too. Invites us to find out more about things, so we can avoid the same grave errors of the past. As the poem and the collection draws to its finale, two questions are asked in the lines 'do you hear me', and 'are you listening'. Penultimate requests, begged. Warnings that come before the very last line, that sums up everything with urgency and painstaking humanity: 're-member me'.

Poetry is undoubtedly the closest language has to magic powers. Audiological and vocal trickery, enchantments, invocations and conjuring, can capture certain states and transmit them. Even across time. Evidently, Juliette Van Der Molen knows this, proving it repeatedly, in this powerful collection. Far from it being whimsical, or dealing in the flim-flam aspects of wordplay and sense of fun to be had in language, the work is very much a solemn document. Moulded that way by careful sculpting, into loud, essential poetry appropriate for the subject matter. The collection is a deeply empathic testament and tribute to innocent people. Many were brutalised due to the effects of hysteria. Worse still, some were killed, their lives stolen. This collection screams out that they mattered then. What's more, it demands that they continue to matter, right now in the present, too.

Contributor Biographies

1. **Allie Kerper** expects to receive her MFA in Creative Writing from the University of Glasgow this winter. Her poetry has previously appeared in SNACK Magazine, SPAM zine, Neon, Adjacent Pineapple and elsewhere. She lives in Edinburgh and works in higher education. You can find her on Twitter at @kerperplexed.

2. **Andrew Geoffrey Kwabena Moss** is a writer and teacher who has lived in the UK, Japan and currently Australia. Of Anglo-Ghanaian heritage, his work seeks to explore and challenge liminal landscapes, complex identities and the social constructs of race. Andrew is a member of the ACT Writers' Centre and has previously had work published by *Afropean, People in Harmony* and *The Word Bin* podcast..

3. **Anita Gracey** is a poet from Belfast. She has been published in reputable journals such as Poetry Ireland Review and has been shortlisted for competitions, most recently Chultúrlann Poetry 2020. Anita is supported by an iDA award, managed by the University of Atypical on behalf of the Arts Council of Northern Ireland.

4. **Benjamin Francis Cassidy** is a 38-year old aspiring writer, who lives in Longsight, Manchester, with his cat, Lucy. Born in Blackpool, he left to seek his fortunes…he doesn't have much money, but did finally get his degree, from Manchester Metropolitan University, graduating in 2018. Since then, he's attended further writing courses and workshops, resulting in getting published in two anthologies of new writing, from Comma Press. He writes non-fiction, too, regularly contributing to Sci-fi-Pulse website, and Mad Hatter Reviews. Previously he's written for Louder Than War music magazine, MCR Live, Haunt Manchester, and has contributed to various blogs. Recently his reviews of poetry and artwork have been accepted by The Lake and High Window. Ben runs Seymour Poets, a community poetry group for vulnerable and struggling adults (he counts himself among them!).

5. **Catherine Davidson** is a British Californian writer who lives in London. She is the author of two pamphlets, *Inheriting the Ocean* (Slow Dancer 1998) and *Behind the Lines* (The Word Hoard 2012); her poems have won recognition on both sides of the Atlantic, including 2017 commendations from The Troubadour International Poetry award and the Free Verse festival. She teaches creative writing to international students at Regent's University and is Chair of the board of Exiled Writer's Ink, where she runs the advanced poetry workshop.

6. **Cheryl Byrne** is a writer based in Manchester who primarily writes Short Stories. Her story, Grimhilde has recently been published in Analogies and Allegories Literary Journal. She is the Head of Community for Orton Publishing and as part of this role, is involved in running Orton's Manchester Writers Circle, a group to support and help writers.

7. **Claire Walker's** most recent publications are Collision (Against the Grain Poetry Press, 2019) and Hierarchy of Needs: A Retelling (V. Press, 2020 - co-authored with Charley Barnes.) Her pamphlet, Somewhere Between Rose and Black (V. Press, 2017) was shortlisted for Best Poetry Pamphlet in the 2018 Saboteur Awards. Claire is co-editor of Atrium poetry webzine.

8. **Damon Moore** manages an artist studios project in Frome, Somerset. Having a particular interest in the narrative style, his shorter form poetry has appeared in journals and magazines including RAUM, Porridge, Wildness and most recently, Fence. He did not double-punch his ticket on the Paris Metro deliberately.

9. **Daniel Hinds** won the Poetry Society's Timothy Corsellis Young Critics Prize and his prose poem review of Jay Bernard's *Surge* was one of the winners of the Shortlist Book Review Competition, held in celebration of the Dylan Thomas Prize. He was shortlisted for the Streetcake Experimental Writing Prize 2019 and the Terry Kelly Poetry Prize 2018. His poetry has been published or is forthcoming in *The London Magazine*, *The New European*, *Wild Court*, *Stand*, *Poetry Birmingham Literary Journal*, *Streetcake Magazine*, *Blackbox Manifold*, *The Honest Ulsterman*, *Finished Creatures*, *Rewilding: An Ecopoetic Anthology*, Newcastle University's *One Planet Anthology*, *Riggwelter*, and elsewhere. Twitter: @DanielGHinds

10. **Fokkina McDonnell** is an established poet with two collections (*Another life,* Oversteps Books Ltd, 2016; *Nothing serious, nothing dangerous,* Indigo Dreams Publishing, 2019) and a pamphlet (*A Stolen Hour*, Grey Hen Press, 2020). Her poems have been widely anthologised, published online and in magazines. She received a Northern Writers' Award from New Writing North in 2020. Twitter: @FokkinaM

11. **Holly Magill** has had poetry in numerous magazines and anthologies. She is co-editor at Atrium – www.atriumpoetry.com. Her first pamphlet, *The Becoming of Lady Flambé*, is available from Indigo Dreams Publishing. https://www.indigodreams.co.uk/holly-magill/4594330527

12. **Jean Gillespie** is a new writer of poetry. Primarily a visual artist, she recently started writing poetry and fell in love with it. She has been working as a visual artist for almost 20 years, having started late because of economic circumstances, and now works with drawing, painting, printmaking and now is experimenting with sound and poetry.

13. **John Winder** is a landscape photographer working mainly in the medium of black and white. He began creative photography 40 years ago and is still surprised by the pleasure of both the act of photography and the resulting images. He enjoys the outdoors, nature and the environment.

14. **Julian Bishop** is a former television journalist living in North London who is a member of the collective group Poets For The Planet. A former runner-up in the Ginkgo Prize for Eco Poetry, he's been shortlisted for the Bridport Poetry Prize and is one of four poets featured in a 2020 pamphlet called Poems For The Planet. He's recently had poems in The Morning Star, XR's Rebel Talk, online journal Irisi, Finished Creatures magazine and the first issue of The Alchemy Spoon. Contact: twitter @julianbpoet Poems For The Planet available at: https://www.maggiebutt.co.uk/poets-for-the-planet

15. **Kevin Bateman** is a Surrealist poet from Galway currently based in his mind who has created at a variety of Events In Spiritual Places That People Have Forgotten To Visit. https://tinyurl.com/Kevin-Bateman-Presents. His mind is a transparency. He has been told his poetry has a surrealist aesthetic quality and is willing to take that at face value as a compliment.

16. **K. James D'Agostino** is an author and poet, and an editorial assistant for the Ninth Letter literary journal. They have a BA from the University of Houston and are currently an MFA candidate at the University of Illinois. Their most recent work has been published in The Gravity Of The Thing and the KAIROS Literary Magazine.

17. **Lee-Ann Coleman** trained as a scientist and worked in scientific administration during the latter part of her career. She is now developing her creative side, exploring the unknown through fiction.

18. **Louise Longson** is an Oxfordshire-based writer, who has been published by *One Hand Clapping*. A qualified psychotherapist, working for a charity serving those distressed by loneliness, she has finally cleared enough of her own head-space and house-space to pursue her writing in earnest. *Twitter @LouisePoetical*

19. **Louise Mather** is a writer and poet from Northern England. You can find her on Twitter @lm2020uk and her work/upcoming work in *Streetcake Magazine, The Cabinet of Heed, Versification, Crow & Cross Keys* and *Idle Ink*. She is currently writing about places, rituals and endometriosis.

20. **Nasrin Parvaz** became a civil rights activist when the Islamic regime took power in 1979. She was arrested in 1982, and spent eight years in prison. Her books are, One Woman's Struggle in Iran, A Prison Memoir, and The Secret Letters from X to A, (Victorina Press 2018). http://nasrinparvaz.org/

21. **Palak Tewary**, an Indian-born Londoner, is a management/finance professional, who along with being an ardent writer, is a travel buff & photography/videography enthusiast. She writes fiction, non-fiction and poetry and has been published in journals, anthologies and online – her blog and published work can be found on www.palaktewary.com. Connect on YouTube/Twitter/ Instagram @palaktewary.

22. **Rebecca Drake** is a poet and PhD student in York. She is the first poet-in-residence at Hull's Maritime Museum, where she is asking at what point people and animals become objects. She has previously been published in The Looking Glass Anthology and in Black bough Magazine.

23. **R.G. Jodah** lives in London and has recently appeared in: PORT (Dunlin Press), Dawntreader, Ink, Sweat & Tears, The Poetry Kit, London Grip

24. **Samuel Strathman** is a poet, author, educator, and the founder/editor-in-chief of Floodlight Editions. His second chapbook, "The Incubus" was published by Roaring Junior Press, 2020. He lives in Toronto, Ontario.

25. **Tim Kiely** is a criminal barrister and poet based in London. His work has featured in 'Lunar Poetry', 'South Bank Poetry', 'Under the Radar' and 'Magma'. His debut pamphlet, 'Hymn to the Smoke', is published by Indigo Dreams.

26. **William Shaw** is a writer from Sheffield, currently living in London. His writing has appeared in *Star*Line, Space & Time*, and *Doctor Who Magazine*. You can find him on Twitter @Will_S_7

New Release Fly on the Wall Press...

Medusa Retold
By Sarah Wallis
£5.99

A feminist retelling of the Medusa myth, set in a run-down, modern seaside town, Medusa Retold is filled with the magic and fury of the original tale. In this telling, loner Nuala is difficult and introverted, fascinated by creatures of the sea. Athena becomes her best friend and first crush, and together they form a duo which is ripped apart by circumstance, leaving Nuala unprotected, unable to save herself. A long-form poem of poignant motifs which recur throughout, the poem is a mythic puzzle, an epic for ordinary girls, and a love letter to the sea. 30 pages.

"Sarah Wallis is a very fine poet and storyteller. She deftly re-inhabits the Medusa myth, losing none of the magic and mystery and yet giving it a contemporary and affecting resonance. She salutes the ancient gods, particularly Athena but also deals with 21st century questions of identity and gender. A miniature epic full of wonderful writing."

> **James Nash, poet, recent collections, "Some Things Matter: 63 Sonnets "(2012); "A Bench for Billie Holiday" (2018), both from Valley Press.**

"A wild and writhing reimagination of the Medusa myth for the modernage. Mesmerising. Compelling."

> **Tanya Shadrick, editor of Wild Woman Swimming.**

"In this vivid retelling of the well-known Greek myth, Wallis captures Medusa's spirit of fury borne of oppression and shapes it into acontemporary story of female rage. Medusa Retold is gripping, raw andessential reading for the modern-day feminist."-

> **JL Corbett, editor Idle Ink**

About Fly on the Wall Press

A publisher with a conscience.
Publishing high quality anthologies on pressing issues, chapbooks and poetry products, from exceptional poets around the globe.
Founded in 2018 by founding editor, Isabelle Kenyon.

Other publications:

Please Hear What I'm Not Saying
Persona Non Grata
Bad Mommy/Stay Mommy by Elisabeth Horan
The Woman With An Owl Tattoo by Anne Walsh Donnelly
the sea refuses no river by Bethany Rivers
White Light White Peak by Simon Corble
Second Life by Karl Tearney
The Dogs of Humanity by Colin Dardis
Small Press Publishing: The Dos and Don'ts by Isabelle Kenyon
Alcoholic Betty by Elisabeth Horan
Awakening by Sam Love
Grenade Genie by Tom McColl
House of Weeds by Amy Kean and Jack Wallington
No Home In This World by Kevin Crowe
How To Make Curry Goat by Louise McStravick
The Goddess of Macau by Graeme Hall
The Prettyboys of Gangster Town by Martin Grey
The Sound of the Earth Singing to Herself by Ricky Ray
Inherent by Lucia Orellana Damacela
Medusa Retold by Sarah Wallis

Social Media:
@fly_press (Twitter)
@flyonthewall_poetry (Instagram)
@flyonthewallpress (Facebook)
www.flyonthewallpress.co.uk